W9-AUI-725

THE
VIKING'S
REVENGE

WARRIOR HEROES

Crabtree Publishing Company

www.crabtreebooks.com

1-800-387-7650

616 Welland Ave.
St. Catharines, ON
L2M 5V6

PMB 59051, 350 Fifth Ave.
59th Floor,
New York, NY

Published by Crabtree Publishing Company in 2015.

Author: Benjamin Hulme-Cross

Illustrator: Angelo Rinaldi

Project coordinator: Kelly Spence

Editors: Alex Van Tol, Kathy Middleton

Proofreader: Wendy Scavuzzo

Prepress technician: Tammy McGarr

Print coordinator: Katherine Berti

Copyright © 2014 A & C Black

Text copyright © 2014 Benjamin Hulme-Cross

Illustration copyright © Angelo Rinaldi

Additional illustrations © Shutterstock

First published 2014 by A & C Black, an imprint of Bloomsbury Publishing Plc.

Printed in Canada/022015/IH20141209

Library and Archives Canada Cataloguing in Publication

Hulme-Cross, Benjamin, author
The Viking's revenge / written by Benjamin Hulme-Cross
; illustrated by Angelo Rinaldi.

(Warrior heroes)
First published 2014 by A & C Black.
ISBN 978-0-7787-1767-6 (bound).--
ISBN 978-0-7787-1771-3 (pbk.)

        I. Rinaldi, Angelo, illustrator II. Title.

PZ7.H87397Vi 2015   j823'.92
C2014-907826-9

Library of Congress Cataloging-in-Publication Data

CIP available at the Library of Congress

THE
VIKING'S
REVENGE

WARRIOR HEROES

BENJAMIN HULME-CROSS

Illustrated by

Angelo Rinaldi

Crabtree Publishing Company
www.crabtreebooks.com

CONTENTS

INTRODUCTION

~ The Hall of Heroes 7

CHAPTER 1 11

~ Thralls 20

CHAPTER 2 23

~ Viking Longhouses 38

CHAPTER 3 41

~ Viking Crime and Punishment 53

CHAPTER 4 55

~ Viking Gods and Goddesses 70

CHAPTER 5 73

~ Viking Weapons 83

CHAPTER 6 87

CHAPTER 7 99

~ Viking Longships 113

CHAPTER 8 117

CHAPTER 9 131

~ Raiders and Berserkers 141

CHAPTER 10 143

INTRODUCTION
THE HALL OF HEROES

The Hall of Heroes is a museum
all about warriors throughout
history. It's full of swords, bows
and arrows, helmets, boats, armor,
shields, spears, axes, and just
about anything else that a warrior
might need. But this isn't just
another museum full of old stuff
in glass cases. It's also haunted
by the ghosts of the warriors whose
belongings are kept there.

Our great-grandfather, Professor
Blade, started the museum. When he
died, his ghost began to haunt the
place, too. He felt guilty about the
trapped ghost warriors and vowed
he would not rest in peace until
all the other ghosts were laid to
rest first. And that's where Arthur
and I come in...

On the night of our great-grandfather's funeral, Arthur and I broke into the museum, for old times' sake. We knew it was wrong, but we just couldn't help ourselves. And that's when we discovered something very weird. When one of the ghost warriors touches either one of us, we get transported back to the time and place where that ghost lived and died. And we can't get back until we've fixed whatever it is that keeps the ghost from resting in peace. So Arthur and I go from one mission to the next, recovering lost swords, avenging deaths, saving loved ones, and doing whatever else these ghost warriors need us to do.

Fortunately, while the Professor

was alive, I wrote down everything
he ever told us about these
warriors in a book I call *Warrior
Heroes*. So we do have some idea of
what we're getting into each time,
even if Arthur does still call me
"Finn the geek." But we need more
than just a book to survive each
adventure, because wherever we go,
we're surrounded by war and battle
and the fiercest fighters who ever
lived—as you're about to find out!

CHAPTER 1

Arthur shivered, wondering where the cruel screeching was coming from. His bones ached from the cold. His face was wet and his nostrils were full of the smells of leaves and mud. He didn't want to wake up. But of course, as soon as you think that, you always do.

Find Blood Hunter!

He rolled over onto his back and opened

his eyes, slowly letting in the thin dawn light. A spider crawled out of his hair and down his cheek. The screeching of birds continued.

"Finn!" he croaked. Looking around, he saw nothing but trees in all directions. *I must be in a forest somewhere,* he thought. He scanned the trees for any sign of his younger brother. Nothing.

Arthur had no idea where he was. He concentrated hard. An image of an old man looking down at him very seriously flashed before his eyes. His name danced around the edges of Arthur's memory.

"Good luck," he said "and be brave." Then another man stepped into view, huge and bearded, wearing a helmet. Arthur's memories rushed into focus: Professor Blade...the Hall of Heroes...the Viking...*Find Blood Hunter!*

Somewhere nearby, a stick snapped. Arthur leaped up into a crouch and turned to face the sound, praying that he would see Finn. A boy peered out curiously from behind a tree. Not Finn. The boy took a startled step back and dropped the wood he was carrying.

"OK," said Arthur, holding both hands up cautiously. "It's OK."

The boy didn't move. He just stared at Arthur with ice-blue eyes. Arthur stared back. It was then he realized it was a girl. Her blonde hair was cut short like a boy's, and she wore a thick metal band around her neck. Her brown clothes were worn and rough, but the face was definitely that of a girl. She didn't speak. She just stared unblinking at Arthur.

Arthur gave her his best reassuring smile,

but this did not have the desired effect. She turned and ran, disappearing into the trees within seconds.

Arthur frowned and brushed some small leaves away from his face. He stood up and stretched and thought for a while about what to do next. He still didn't have a clue where he was or where Finn was. With no better ideas, he soon began to walk in the direction that the girl had run.

He had taken barely three steps when he heard a hiss and a thud. An arrow, still quivering in the ground, had appeared at Arthur's feet. He jumped back, and another arrow hissed into the earth to his right. He leaped behind a tree and waited for the attackers to show themselves.

Soon, the girl emerged from the trees. She was being pushed along by a huge, red-faced boy.

Another boy followed with an arrow notched ready in his bow.

"You there!" shouted the boy with the bow. "My name is Brand Hallvardson, and this forest belongs to my father."

"Get out from behind that tree, coward!" yelled Red-face.

"I have no weapons, and I mean you no harm," Arthur called back.

"No talking. I said show yourself!" The boy was shouting so loud that his voice cracked.

Slowly, Arthur stepped out from behind the tree. Brand Hallvardson looked straight at him along his notched arrow.

"Thorfinna here says you were sleeping in the forest," said Brand, nodding at the girl. "Who are you?"

"I'm nobody, really," Arthur replied. "My name is Arthur. But I'm just passing through. I didn't know this was your father's land."

"Where are you from?" Brand asked, eyeing Arthur's clothes suspiciously.

Always a difficult question. "A long way from here," said Arthur.

"If that's your best answer, then you're coming with us," said Brand. "My father could use another thrall to work the fields. Thorfinna, stay back. Olaf, go and get him."

The red-faced boy smirked and walked up to Arthur and stood right in front of him.

"I'm going to enjoy punishing this thrall." He clenched his fists and pulled his arm back to punch Arthur in the stomach. But, just as Olaf swung his fist toward him, Arthur stepped back.

Olaf staggered forward, following the force of his punch.

"Stay where you are!" Brand yelled, his bow still drawn. But now Olaf was between him and Arthur, blocking Brand's shot. Arthur dropped his shoulder and crunched it into Olaf's chest, driving him back toward the landowner's son.

Brand leaped to the side, and Arthur spun Olaf around to block the shot again. Olaf screamed in pain, clutching at the arrow that was now lodged in his arm, spilling blood onto the forest floor. He stumbled backward. Brand was notching up a second arrow. Arthur gave Olaf a mighty shove in the stomach. He flew back into Brand, and they both crashed to the ground.

The bow was knocked from Brand's grasp, and Arthur dived for it. Olaf knelt on the ground, moaning and clutching at his wound. But Brand was on his feet in a moment, a knife grasped in one hand and a stick in the other. Arthur held the bow in both hands like a sword, and the two circled warily, their eyes locked together, each one waiting for the other to move first. Brand's eyes flickered slightly, glancing over

Arthur's shoulder for a split second. *An old trick*, thought Arthur—not one he was about to fall for.

That was when Arthur felt an explosion of pain in the back of his skull.. The world tipped over, as his head erupted into tiny points of light, and his legs gave way from beneath him. He was unconscious before he hit the ground.

EXTRACT FROM *WARRIOR HEROES*
BY FINN BLADE

THRALLS

Vikings called their slaves
thralls. Slavery was big business
for the Vikings. They captured
thralls in battle, kidnapped them
on raids, or created them by
condemning criminals to slavery.
Most families had at least one
thrall. Some had as many as thirty.
In fact, the Vikings traded in
thralls more than anything else.

SO WHAT DOES IT MEAN TO BE A VIKING THRALL?

THE GOOD
• Your master is expected to look
  after you if you are unwell.

- Your master is allowed to free you if he wants to.

- It's possible to buy your freedom if you can pay your master what he would get if he were to sell you.

THE BAD

- You'll get the worst, most back-breaking jobs going.

- You won't get paid.

- You won't have much time to try to make any money on the side—and that's your only hope of buying your freedom.

- To mark you as a thrall, you are fitted with a metal collar that is welded on. If you escape, everyone will know you are a thrall.

- If you escape and get caught, you'll be killed instantly.

- Your master is allowed to kill you whenever he feels like it, without being punished.

Weighed out, not a great life, and it's almost impossible to escape.

CHAPTER 2

A short distance away, Finn woke to hear Arthur calling out.

Finn hated the first few minutes in a new time. He was always separated from Arthur. They had agreed many times that, when they woke up somewhere new, they would stay hidden from anyone else until they found each other. Yet somehow, Arthur always managed to cause a whole heap of trouble before Finn found him.

Sure enough, the shouts and thuds of a fight reached Finn's ears. Quelling a mixture of anger and panic, he pulled himself up from where he was lying and ran uphill through the trees toward the noise.

As he reached the top of the sloping ground, he caught sight of the boys. A red-faced boy lay on the forest floor, clutching at an arrow in his arm, while Arthur and another boy circled each other close by. Just as Finn began to creep forward, an old man holding a long walking staff appeared behind Arthur. Before Finn could shout a warning, the man's staff had connected with the back of Arthur's head, and Arthur dropped to the ground with a heavy thud.

Finn froze, one hand over his mouth. He

was torn between his natural caution and the desperate urge to help his brother. The old man calmly walked over to look at the boy's injury.

Finn's caution won over. He would be no use to Arthur if he were caught, too, he reasoned. As quietly as he could, he stepped behind a tree and crouched down out of sight.

A few moments later, the old man picked Arthur up, threw him across his shoulder, and began to walk. The two boys followed, arguing about something that Finn couldn't quite hear.

Finn stepped out from behind the tree, but immediately froze. A girl about his own age had appeared with the group. Just as Finn had broken cover, she turned and looked straight at him. She had blue eyes and wore a metal collar. *A thrall*, thought Finn, remembering what he had researched for his *Warrior Heroes* journal.

Furious with himself for being spotted, Finn was about to run when the girl put a finger to her lips and reached out a hand toward him, as though telling him to stop.

"Thorfinna!" someone barked.

The girl dropped her hand and turned quickly to follow the rest of her group through the trees.

Finn was now completely unsure how to proceed. Arthur had been knocked out and carried off, and one of Arthur's captors, albeit a thrall, had discovered Finn watching. If he stayed where he was, he might lose Arthur. If he followed, then the thrall might alert the others. Finn rubbed his eyes and looked up at the sky. When he looked back toward the trees, the thrall, Arthur, and his captors had disappeared.

That helped Finn make up his mind. He couldn't just stand by and do nothing. As quietly as possible, he jogged through the trees after Arthur. In a few minutes, he came to a stop at the edge of the forest. Finn quickly hid himself behind a tree. Looking ahead, he saw the group walking toward a long, curved-roof building surrounded by fields and a few small huts. *A Viking longhouse*, Finn thought. Once again, the thrall turned and looked straight at him. Again, she put a finger to her lips. But, this time, she smiled.

The old man carried Arthur into one of the huts, then re-emerged, shutting and bolting the door behind him. Finn turned and walked back deeper into the forest. Now that he knew where they were keeping Arthur, he felt a little better.

All he needed to do was wait until nightfall, then let Arthur out of the building. And the thrall appeared to be on his side, which was a very welcome bit of luck.

Finn found a tall pine tree, climbed high up into its branches, and made himself as comfortable as he could. Settling down for a long wait, he allowed his mind to wander back to the Hall of Heroes.

* * *

Finn and Arthur had been telling the Professor all about their last adventure, when the air in the room seemed to shift, as though trying to flatten itself against the walls.

"Boys, he's coming!" The Professor looked at the door of his study. Finn felt the familiar nervous knot in his stomach. Where would they be sent this time?

The sound of slow, heavy footsteps thudded along the corridor outside, growing louder as somebody approached the study.

The lamp on the Professor's desk flickered and went out. Complete darkness surrounded them. The door handle shook. The door hissed open, then closed again. The boys didn't dare breathe. A few silent moments passed, then a voice that seemed too deep to be human growled, "Find Blood Hunter!"

Silence again. Still the boys did not dare breathe.

The scrape of a match broke the spell. First the match, then a candle, flared into light.

The sight in front of them sucked the breath

out of each boy. Standing before them was a giant of a man. A thick mane of reddish-blond hair escaped from beneath a simple metal helmet. His long, red beard was forked and braided. His eyes were fierce and blue. One of his arms was hidden by a round, painted wooden shield. In his other hand, he held a battle-ax. A Viking!

"They came in the night," the warrior growled. "They killed us, and they took Blood Hunter, my sword. It was my father's sword before me, and his father's before him."

The Professor cleared his throat. "My dear chap," he began. "Do you mean to say that the loss of your sword is the reason you cannot rest? These boys will find your sword but–"

"Yes!" the huge man thundered, his eyes flashing. "They must find it. I have waited

more than a thousand years. The honor of my ancestors depends on it."

"But you will have to tell us a little more about what happened," the Professor resumed. "Who took your sword? Where did they steal it from?"

"The cowards came in the night," the warrior repeated. The man's voice was little more than an anguished whisper now. "They came to the farm, and they killed us all. I woke too late to defend my family. I do not know who they were. But their weapons were like ours. They were not from over the sea."

"Then you were raided by your own kind?" the Professor asked.

"My kind? *My kind?*" the Viking boomed. "They were thieves in the night, and we were warriors. They had no honor. I am Hallvard

Forkbeard. Blood Hunter should be in my hand or in my son's hand, had he lived."

The Professor turned to address the boys. "Hallvard's spirit will only be laid to rest when his sword is returned to him or to his son. Find the sword and he will find peace. But remember, the Vikings valued two things above all else: bravery and honor. Show strength, show courage. But if you do anything behind someone's back and get caught, they will be merciless. Good luck," he concluded. "And be brave."

Finn looked at Arthur fearfully. Even Arthur looked nervous this time.

The Professor looked at the Viking and beckoned. The boys shrank back into the shadows as the warrior stepped forward and placed a large hand on each of their heads.

Mist filled the room, swirling around the boys. The candle flickered out, and plunged them into darkness once more.

* * *

The light was beginning to fade in the forest. *At least I won't have to sit here much longer,* Finn thought, as he shifted uncomfortably in the tree. The branch he was sitting on creaked. He shifted again, and with a sudden snap, the branch gave way sending him crashing to the ground. The birds of the forest shrieked. Finn gasped a curse. Someone giggled. Shaking the sense back into his head, Finn stood up and found himself face to face with the thrall.

"Where did you come from?" he blurted, stumbling backward in surprise.

"Me? I came along the path. Where did you come from?" The girl looked up at the tree, puzzled and amused.

"You haven't said anything to them about me, have you?" Finn asked quickly.

She shook her head. "I'm Thorfinna. You are?"

"Uh, my name's Finn. Why have your friends taken my brother away?"

The girl scowled. "My friends?" she said, fingering the metal band around her neck. "They are *not* my friends. And I'm not going to help them put these collars on anyone else."

"Well, thanks," he said. "But why are you here?"

"Haven't you been listening? I don't want you and your brother to become thralls like me. And if that means helping you both to escape, then so be it," Thorfinna replied.

This was turning out very well indeed, thought Finn.

"Do you know what they're going to do with him? I was planning to go and let him out of the hut after dark. Will there be anyone guarding him or anything?"

"I really do want to help you," said Thorfinna, ignoring Finn's question, "but there is one thing I have to ask in return."

Oh dear, thought Finn. *If something seems too good to be true...*

"What's that, then?" he asked warily.

"Take me with you," said the girl.

Finn thought for a moment. This was a bad idea for so many reasons. He'd be stealing a thrall from the Vikings. The three of them would have to go on the run and never come back. They couldn't hang around and find

Blood Hunter. And even if they did find Blood Hunter, he and Arthur would then wake up in the 21st century, leaving Thorfinna on her own to be caught and killed as an escaped thrall.

Thorfinna studied Finn's face carefully. "Or would you prefer I go back and tell my masters about the second strange boy who's running around in the woods?" she said slyly.

"I don't have much choice, do I?" muttered Finn. "What do you want us to do after we escape?"

"I have a score to settle," Thorfinna replied darkly. "Just get me away from here, and I'll leave you as soon as I've gotten rid of my collar. Deal?"

Finn nodded.

"Good," said the girl. "Wait here. I'll come back at sunset when the others are eating. We'll get your brother then." With that, she walked away.

EXTRACT FROM *WARRIOR HEROES*
BY FINN BLADE

VIKING LONGHOUSES

Life in a Viking longhouse was
pretty basic. The longhouse itself
was made of wood, sometimes with a
roof covered in turf. They ranged
in length from 49 to 246 feet (15
to 75 meters). They were wider in
the middle than at the ends, so the
curved walls made the houses look
a bit like boats.

To preserve heat, there were
often no windows, though some had
small, hide-covered openings near
the roof. This meant that most
light came from fires that burned
in pits on the earthen floor of
the house, or from fish oil lamps.
It also meant that the insides of

longhouses could get very smoky,
though the smoke would drift out
eventually through small smoke-
holes in the roof.

Most people slept on benches that
lined the walls of the longhouse,
probably cushioned by heather
and animal skins. Privacy didn't
exist because a lot of people slept
in one big room: mom, dad, kids,
grandparents, uncles and aunts,
cousins, and thralls. In the winter,
the animals slept inside, too!

CHAPTER 3

By the time the sun set, Finn had convinced himself that helping Thorfinna to escape was a good idea. He needed to get Arthur out, and that would only happen with Thorfinna's help. It also occurred to Finn that having an ally, even if it was just a slave, increased their chances of finding Blood Hunter without getting killed.

He waited nervously for the girl to come for him, but as twilight gave way to almost total darkness, Finn became more and more agitated. He had been waiting in the dark for about an hour by the time he decided that something was wrong. The girl obviously hadn't told her masters about him, but it didn't look as though she was going to come back either. He had no choice. He would have to get Arthur out on his own.

Finn crept through the trees, straining his ears to pick up every strange sound of the forest. A stick snapped up ahead and he froze. Something large with four legs and luminous eyes crossed the path in front of him. Telling himself to get a grip, Finn pressed ahead trying to ignore the pack of ravenous wolves that his imagination was busy dreaming up. He reached the edge of the trees without incident, and gazed over at the settlement. The moon shone brightly, and he could see Arthur's hut clearly.

He could also hear voices coming from the longhouse in the distance. A faint glow at the top of the longhouse lit up the smoke coming from a fireplace inside. Other than that, there was no light to be seen, and Finn concluded that the doors must be closed for the night.

Crouching low, Finn scurried across the grass toward the hut. He covered the distance quickly, and in no time, he was unbolting the door. He opened it carefully and peered inside. He couldn't see a thing. Cautiously, he took a step forward into the pitch-black hut.

Without warning, a fist connected with his chin knocking him to the ground. Somebody jumped on him and grabbed his throat.

"Arthur," he choked. "It's me, Finn!"

"Finn?"

"Yes, you maniac! I'm here to get you out!" he gasped.

Arthur let go of Finn's throat and stood up. "Well, what took you so long?"

"What?" Finn yelped, rubbing his now very sore neck and heaving himself off the floor of the hut. "You started a fight as soon as you got here. You got yourself locked up. And you're complaining that *I'm* late? You're unbelievable. And you *hit* me!"

"Well you should have said it was you," said Arthur, unapologetically. "Anyway, you're here now, and we're good to go. What's the plan?"

Finn looked incredulously at his brother. But

he knew arguing wouldn't get them anywhere. Finn explained what had happened with Thorfinna. Arthur chuckled. "So you've been making friends with girls while I've been locked up, have you? Very nice."

"Shut up, Arthur," said Finn, grateful for the darkness as he blushed. "All you've done is get yourself caught."

"OK, OK," Arthur went on. "Here's what I think. Tomorrow morning they'll come and find I'm gone. They'll know somebody must have opened the door for me, and they'll be on guard. So any chance we had of finding that sword before the thieves take it will be gone."

"So what do we do?" asked Finn.

"We need to find Blood Hunter tonight, before they notice I'm missing."

"No way," said Finn, frowning. "If Hallvard lives in that longhouse, then that's where the sword will be—along with about twenty other people. And it will probably be locked up."

Arthur stared at his brother. "How do you know all this stuff?"

"I listen when people talk to me. You should try it sometime," Finn replied. "The Professor told us all about Vikings living in longhouses."

"Well, we still have to try before it's too late," said Arthur. "Let's find a window and see where everything is. Then I'll creep in after they've all gone to sleep."

Before Finn could answer, Arthur stepped out of the hut and jogged noiselessly across the grass toward the longhouse. Finn followed, muttering under his breath.

As they approached the longhouse, the voices inside grew louder, and they began to make out some of what was being said.

"... just a boy..."

"... old enough to be traveling..."

"... fought with our boys..."

"Oh, great," Finn whispered. "They're arguing about you."

"Quiet!" Arthur commanded as they reached the wall of the longhouse. Firewood was piled up along the wall, and Arthur carefully climbed up on top of the stack. He waved for Finn to follow. From there, they could see a few thin strips across the top of the wall. They might be covered windows, but they were still well out of reach.

Arthur placed his back against the wall with his legs bent like he was sitting on a chair. He pointed at Finn, then tapped his shoulder. Reluctantly, Finn stepped forward. Arthur cupped his hands to make a foothold. Finn stepped from Arthur's hands to his shoulders, then stood up, sliding his chest up the wall until his chin was in line with the bottom of one of the strips they had seen. Sure enough, it seemed to be a small window, covered inside by a piece of animal hide. Finn found the cord that held the hide in place, and began to untie it.

"What can you see?" Arthur whispered.

"Nothing yet," Finn replied, looking down at his brother crossly. His weight shifted slightly on Arthur's shoulders, and Arthur moved his foot. A piece of firewood clattered noisily down the stack, and the voices inside stopped. Finn and Arthur froze.

"Nothing to fear there," somebody growled. "Thorfinna is halfway through moving the wood stack. Some of it is just loose."

Finn let out a quiet sigh of relief and carried on untying the hide as the conversation inside resumed. A corner came loose. Finn pulled it up gently and peered inside the huge building. It was more like a barn than a house. Most of it was one big hall.

In the middle of the floor was a large open fire that sent sweet-smelling smoke circling around the house and up toward a hole in the roof. All the people in the hall were clustered around the fire. Fifteen or so tall, strong-looking, bearded men stood in front forming a circle. Right away, Finn recognized Hallvard's huge frame. Behind the men stood Thorfinna and a group containing some older men, women, and children. Finn had been expecting to see a big family and a few thralls, but this group of men clearly represented more than one family.

"Hallvard called us here to talk, but now he does not want to listen," one man was saying. "The matter is simple. The boy is a stranger. He attacked your son, Hallvard, and Siggurd's son also. You must kill him."

"In the boy's defense, he fought—and bravely, mind you—only when he was attacked and outnumbered," said another. Finn recognized him as the old man who had knocked Arthur out in the forest.

"We would have defeated him in a few more moments, Father," said the boy, defensively.

"Well, perhaps we will put that to the test

in the morning, my son," Hallvard rumbled. "Siggurd, your son now has his first war wound. Be proud."

Finn remembered he was supposed to be looking for the sword, and he scanned the hall. He peered though the swirling smoke. He could make out a collection of spears and bows leaning against the wall in a sort of porch. Wide benches covered in sheepskins lined both sides of the hall. At the hall's other end, he saw a raised platform with a wooden frame and more sheepskins. *Hallvard's bed*, Finn thought.

"Finn!" Arthur whispered.

"OK, I'm coming down," said Finn. "Keep your shirt on."

"Finn, look behind you," Arthur urged, a note of panic in his voice.

Finn turned his head and his blood froze. Someone was holding a long spear to Arthur's throat. The hooded figure spat out a single word.

"Thieves!"

VIKING CRIME AND PUNISHMENT

The Vikings were a proud bunch. You had to be seen to be brave. Bravery brought honor. Cowardice brought dishonor.

So if you snuck up on someone and stole their favorite knife while they weren't looking, you were a thief and a coward. The person you had stolen from had every right to kill you, and would not be punished for it.

On the other hand, if you walked up to them and said "Hey, Eric! Give me that knife!" then you snatched it, they couldn't kill you because you were not being cowardly.

The same went for killing people. Creep up on someone you didn't like and bash them over the head while they were fishing, and you were branded a cowardly murderer.

Shove them around a bit first and shout in their face before bashing them over the head, and you were brave.

For the cowardly crimes, you would be outlawed, which meant you had to go and live in the wilderness. Anyone who just wanted to do a bit of hunting could come along and kill you.

For the so-called "brave" crimes, you normally had to pay compensation to the victim or their family.

Of course, none of this applied to raiding enemies in war. You could sneak up on them and kill them, and still be remembered as a great warrior.

CHAPTER 4

The hood slipped back.

"So, the thrall has a little helper," snarled Olaf. "*Hallvard!*"

The boys found themselves cowering before the furious stares of a large group of full-grown Viking warriors.

"Down!" Hallvard ordered. Shaking, Finn leaped off Arthur's shoulders and clattered down onto the wood stack, which shook and sent the boys sprawling to the ground.

"Arm yourselves," Hallvard growled, and moments later each Viking was brandishing a weapon.

Hallvard snatched Arthur up off the ground and held him in the air by the throat. "How many more of you are there?" he barked.

"It's just us, sir," Arthur squeaked.

"*Liars!*" Hallvard bellowed. "You were spying on us, hiding like rats. Who sent you?" The grip on Arthur's throat tightened and he started to kick his feet. Olaf grinned.

"It's not what you think," Finn blurted. "We came to warn you. Raiders are coming. You must defend yourselves!"

Hallvard dropped Arthur, and the boy

crumpled onto the damp earth, gasping for air. The huge Viking's eyes narrowed as he turned to Finn. "And how would you know that?"

"Blood Hunter!" Finn spluttered.

Hallvard's face paled. "What did you just say, boy?"

"Blood Hunter," Finn repeated desperately, the words tumbling out of his mouth. "We have no chief. Odin is our master. He shows me things. He showed me your sword, Blood Hunter, and he showed me the raid that was coming."

Hallvard threw back his head and roared with laughter. "So two boys spying in the night are Odin's messengers? Do you have names?"

"I'm Finn, and that's my older brother, Arthur." Finn pointed feebly to where Arthur still lay shaking on the ground.

"Good. I like to know people's names if I am going to kill them."

"Be careful, Hallvard," said the old man, stepping forward. "A message from Odin should not be ignored."

"Ragnar, do you really think that these two runts would be the messengers that Odin chooses?"

"You lose nothing by keeping them alive," Ragnar replied, his face deadly serious.

"What?" Olaf snorted. "They attacked us, and you caught them spying!"

"The two of *you* attacked *him*," said Ragnar. "And he had the better of both of you, until I came along."

"Father, may I–" began Brand.

"Enough!" Hallvard barked.

"Father, please," Brand insisted. "Ragnar is right.

When he fought, it was in defense. I don't believe he wanted to fight."

"How can you say that?" Olaf whined, putting a hand where the arrow had pierced him earlier.

"Be quiet, Olaf," said Brand. "He attacked because you tried to punch him. And missed."

"They are spies!" cried Olaf.

"*Enough!*" Hallvard boomed. "My mind is made up. I do not believe that these boys are messengers from Odin. But as Ragnar says, it costs us nothing to keep them alive for a few days. If there is no raid, then the boys are lying. And if there is a raid, they are probably spies for the enemy, in which case they will be useful to us. We will know soon enough."

Another one of the men spoke up. "Hallvard, if raiders are coming, we must defend our families." The others murmured their agreement.

"Quite so," said Hallvard. "Each man must go to his farm and prepare to defend it. If any of us is attacked by more than three men, they must sound the signal, and all others will come to his aid."

"What about the boys?" asked Ragnar.

"Tie them to the tree," Hallvard replied, curtly. "Odin will protect them, if they speak the truth. The rest of you, return to your farms. And fear not, we will defend one another."

Most of the men began to hurry away. Hallvard returned to the longhouse. Ragnar and Brand used spears to shepherd the boys toward a lone tree in the middle of the field.

Brand pulled Arthur's arms roughly behind his back and tied them together, then did the same to Finn. When he had finished, he pushed both boys against the tree and looped each rope around the trunk tightly.

It was clear that there was little to be gained from fighting, and neither boy said a word, until Brand asked, "So did Odin tell you this would happen?"

"He never really says much about the danger we'll be in," Finn replied, glumly.

Ragnar chuckled. "Well, you have a dangerous night ahead of you, boys. You will need Odin's protection from the bears and wolves tonight, not to mention from Hallvard in the morning." With that, he beckoned to Brand, and the pair hurried back to the longhouse.

Arthur pulled forward with one arm, tugging Finn tighter against the tree.

"Stop it, you're hurting me!" Finn croaked.

"Boohoo," said Arthur. "We have to find a way of getting loose."

"Well, if you had just listened to me, we wouldn't be in this mess."

"If I'd listened to you, we wouldn't be anywhere," Arthur snapped. "We had no choice but to look for Blood Hunter. And why did you tell Hallvard that we knew about his sword?"

"I had to say something," said Finn, outraged. "He was going to kill us!"

But Arthur wasn't finished. "I can't believe you said we were here because Odin told us there would be a raid... Who is Odin, anyway?"

"He's one of their gods. Again, you should try that "listening to people" thing we talked about earlier. And I didn't hear any better ideas

from you," Finn snarled. "At least we're still alive."

"For now," said Arthur. "But not for much longer if we stay tied to this tree. Come on, let's try to rub the rope against the tree to see if we can cut through it."

The boys pulled and tugged, but all they got for their efforts were rope burns and worse tempers. They gave up. For a while, neither of them spoke. Then Arthur thought of something.

"Hey, there's one good thing. At least now Hallvard is on guard against the raiders."

"How does that help us?" Finn wondered.

"Back at The Hall of Heroes, Hallvard's ghost said his whole family was killed in the night because they weren't ready. Now they're ready, aren't they?" Arthur tugged at the rope again. "Maybe now he won't lose his sword or be killed.

This could be easier than we thought!"

"Well, we won't know until the raid happens," said Finn. "And I don't know about you, but I'm not a fan of being tied to a tree when a bunch of Viking raiders turn up planning to kill everyone."

The image hung heavily in the air.

"Let's try the ropes again," Arthur said.

They sawed rope against bark. They twisted their hands trying to reach the knots. They squeezed fingers together and tried to slip their hands out of the bonds. All for nothing. Exhausted and painfully bruised, their heads drooping forward, they gave up. Time passed slowly. As the heat from their exertions faded, both boys began to shiver. Strange noises from the forest began to fill the air. Neither had anything to say to cheer the other up, and it seemed to both that their situation could not be much worse.

Finn's mind drifted to the Professor and the Hall of Heroes. *What do we do now?* he silently implored.

Then, from somewhere beyond the longhouse, they heard the distant blast of a horn.

Arthur's head snapped up. "What was that?"

They heard shouts from the longhouse.

"Hallvard told the men to signal if they were attacked," said Finn.

"What do we do?" Arthur hissed. "Come on, you're the brainy one."

"I don't know."

"Pssst!"

"What?"

"That wasn't me."

Suddenly, Thorfinna emerged from the darkness and dropped a bunch of items on the ground at Finn's feet. She pointed a knife in his direction and stared hard at him.

"How did you know about the raiders?" she demanded.

"What?" said Finn. "Does it matter? Why didn't you come back to meet me in the forest, like you said you would?"

"I couldn't get away," said Thorfinna, tersely. "How did you know about the raiders? It matters a lot if you're one of them."

"There's no time for explanations," Finn countered. "Cut us loose or we'll be slaughtered. I'll tell you if I get a chance."

"How do I know you won't kill me as soon as

I cut you loose?" Thorfinna was still staring hard at him.

"Surely you know you can trust us," Arthur cut in. "If he wanted to kill you, he could have done it when he saw you in the forest. Please! That's why you came here, isn't it? To cut us loose?"

"I came because I thought now would be a good time to run," said Thorfinna.

"No!" Finn said, abruptly. "If we run, they'll think we were with the raiders. They'll come after us and kill us. We prove ourselves by staying and fighting."

Thorfinna thought for a few moments.

"You might be right," she said, stepping forward. She began to cut through the ropes. "But when the time comes, you remember that I saved your lives. I set *you* free—you set *me* free. Hallvard is a good man and treats me well enough, but I have deaths to avenge, and I can't do that here."

VIKING GODS AND GODDESSES

The Vikings believed in a huge
number of gods and goddesses, as
well as a host of strange beings
including frost giants, dwarves,
immortal wolves, elves, and
numerous terrifying beasts and
monsters. These are the two most
important gods for Viking warriors:

ODIN

The god of magic, poetry, and war,
Odin is the top god, and he got
there in a grisly way. Rumor has
it he hung himself from a gallows
tree for nine days and nights to
learn how to read and write. They
also say he gave one of his eyes in
return for the chance to drink from

the well of knowledge. He is often seen hanging around with wolves and ravens, looking like a strange old wizard leaning on a staff. He has a magic spear that never misses its target, and since he is the god of war, there are plenty of stories about him using it!

THOR

Thor is the god of thunder. He is extremely brave, and extremely strong, but not too bright. He has long red hair, a big red beard, a magic belt that increases his strength, and a huge hammer. And as if that's not enough, he gets to roam around the skies in a chariot. The wheels of the chariot create thunder, and when Thor throws his hammer, lightning blazes across the sky.

VALHALLA

Viking warriors believe that if they die bravely in battle, then the Valkyries, who are Odin's warrior-maidens, will carry them away to Odin's Hall, called Valhalla. Valhalla is a sort of Viking heaven, where warriors spend the afterlife feasting with Odin and telling stories.

CHAPTER 5

Arthur stepped away from the tree, free at last.

"What's happening?" he asked, rubbing his bruised wrists. "How many people are there?"

"Hallvard sent people to different places to watch for raiders. Brand was at the beach, and it was him who blew the horn," Thorfinna said, pointing past the longhouse. "If they know where they're going, the raiders will be here first. Our friends from the other farms will take longer. Here, I brought weapons." Thorfinna had placed an ax, a bow, and some arrows on the floor.

"If we're not running away, then I'm going back to the longhouse," Thorfinna told them. "It's up to you what you do now." She turned and sped away.

"Quick," said Arthur. "We need to impress Hallvard and win his trust. You're the expert archer. Let's get you up on the roof of the longhouse, and you can be a sort of sniper."

Finn was used to Arthur taking charge when fighting broke out. He didn't argue. They gathered up the weapons Thorfinna had brought, and raced over to the longhouse and up onto the wood stack. Arthur helped Finn up as he had done earlier that evening, and Finn pulled himself up onto the roof.

"What are you going to do?" he whispered down to his brother.

Arthur grinned. "I'm going to see if I can sink the raiders' boat. If that doesn't impress Hallvard, nothing will!"

Finn opened his mouth to reply, but before he could say anything, Arthur had jumped from the longhouse and disappeared into the night.

The longhouse stood beside a path that Finn presumed led in the direction of the sea. He took up a position just below the top of the roof so that, when he peered over the roof's ridge, he could see a good distance along the path.

Finn could hear Hallvard barking orders in the longhouse. It was clear to Finn that he planned to get everyone into the trees for safety, then set an ambush for the raiders.

The people inside needed no encouragement, and in no time at all the house stood empty. Looking down, Finn saw Ragnar leading a small party of women, children, and old men away from the farm and back toward the woods where he and Arthur had first arrived. There was no sign of Thorfinna.

Meanwhile, Hallvard was calling out orders to three other men. Moments later, they vanished into the trees on both sides of the path.

For a short while, the only sounds that Finn could hear were the occasional cries of wild animals. Then, very faintly at first but growing louder and louder, came the thundering sound of men running.

Finn's heartbeat quickened. He notched his first arrow and stared along the moonlit path.

The sound of running stopped.

Silence. Finn drew the bowstring back.

Shadowy figures began to emerge as about twenty Viking raiders crept out from the trees. They held huge, wooden shields in front of them, and swords, spears, and axes at the ready.

Finn waited. *Why isn't Hallvard attacking?* The men crept closer. Finn stared along his arrow. *Should I fire first?*

A shout went up from the back of the group of raiders. *"Ambush!"*

Two of the men at the back of the group fell to the ground, arrows sticking out of their necks.

Finn fired his first arrow, and a third raider went down. *This might actually work!*

But the raiders reacted quickly, and those that remained scattered into the woods on both sides of the path. From the shouts and the loud clatter of the wooden shields, Finn guessed that Hallvard's men were now engaged in close fighting in the trees.

Finn kept his eyes on the path. Suddenly Hallvard leaped backward onto the path, pursued by one of the raiders. Their swords flashed in the moonlight. Hallvard smashed the edge of his shield into the raider's face and lunged forward, burying his sword in the man. Hallvard kicked the crumpled raider backward onto the path.

Two more raiders appeared as if from nowhere to replace the fallen man. They swung at Hallvard, who ducked and parried but was driven back toward the longhouse. Finn fired another arrow, and it whistled past Hallvard and into the chest of one of his attackers, who fell to the ground.

Yet again, the fallen man was replaced by two more raiders. Now Hallvard found himself facing three men. Finn fired again as one of the raiders took a huge swing at Hallvard with an ax. The arrow missed its mark. Hallvard blocked the blow from the ax with his shield, but was forced down on one knee as the shield splintered and cracked above him.

The man brought his ax up once more, but then dropped to his knees with a scream. As he fell forward, Finn could see an ax protruding from the man's back.

Shouts rang out, and a new group ran toward Hallvard. Reinforcements from the farms! The two remaining raiders turned and disappeared into the trees, with Hallvard's allies in hot pursuit.

Finn almost laughed with relief, but his joy was premature. Two more raiders emerged from the trees near the longhouse and ran forward. Finn's heart raced. He quickly brought one of the men down with an arrow. The second raider looked straight up at where the arrow had come from, and spotted Finn. The boy froze as the man bared his teeth. In a split-second, the raider sent an ax spinning through the air toward Finn's throat.

Instinctively, Finn ducked as the ax whistled overhead. Losing his footing, he slid down the roof and crashed onto the wood stack. Winded, he scrambled to his feet and saw the ax buried in the ground. He staggered over to it and desperately tried to yank it free. A snarl made him

look up. His stomach lurched. The ax thrower had rounded the corner of the longhouse and was running toward him, his face twisting with rage. He held a sword aloft in one hand, and roared as he charged.

Finn wrenched frantically at the ax. The raider was almost on him. His palms slipped on the handle of the ax, and once again, he ended up on the ground, face first, just as the raider reached him. Surprised by Finn's fall, the huge man tripped and fell directly on top of him. He felt the raider begin to lift himself. *This is the end*, Finn thought. *I wonder if dying here means I'll go to Valhalla...*

The raider struggled to lift his weight off Finn, then he grunted and collapsed back on top of the boy. Finn felt a warm liquid flowing down his neck.

Death wasn't so painful.

Then the weight of the raider was gone entirely. Finn rolled limply onto his back, gazing up. Standing over him was a giant of a man.

"Maybe you are Odin's chosen one," said Hallvard, pulling a sword from the raider's back.

EXTRACT FROM *WARRIOR HEROES*
BY FINN BLADE

VIKING WEAPONS

Here's a list of all the kit the well-prepared Viking needs.

SWORD

A sword is a Viking's most precious possession—so much so that it is often given a name. It marks the owner as a warrior and offers him the chance to win glory and honor on the battlefield. The Viking sword is a double-edged blade made of iron, sometimes with steel edges. It is about 30 inches (75 cm) long and 2 inches (5 cm) wide. The sword's edge is more dangerous than the point. It is used more for slicing than stabbing.

SHIELD

The shield is made of wood. It is up to 3 feet (1 meter) across, so it can be used as an attacking weapon as well as in defense. It is often painted in simple patterns.

AX

Not every man has a sword, but most have axes. Axes are made of iron, with wooden handles. They can be used in battle to chop, but can also be thrown to bring down an enemy from a short distance.

SPEAR

Also made with an iron head and a wooden handle. If you can't afford a sword, you should definitely carry a spear. You probably won't use it for throwing, but more for thrusting and stabbing so that you can reach your enemy before he can reach you.

BOW

Bows and arrows are normally used for hunting rather than battle, though they do have their uses in some fighting situations. Bows are generally made from yew, and are nearly as tall as a man.

ARMOR

Wealthy chieftans might have chain mail and round iron helmets, but most Viking warriors make do with leather helmets and armor. Nobody has ever heard of a real Viking wearing a helmet with horns, so get that idea out of your head!

CHAPTER 6

It was a hushed, stunned group that gathered in the longhouse to wait for dawn. Ragnar's party had returned from hiding. Two of Hallvard's men had died in the battle, one of them leaving behind a wife and two young children who huddled, red-eyed, in a corner with his body. The men from the farms had chased the raiders toward the sea, but neither they nor

Brand nor Arthur had returned to the longhouse.

Hallvard paced back and forth in front of the fire pit, nostrils flared, teeth clenched, the flames flicking shadows across his face. One woman sat opposite him, but nobody else dared approach. At last, the woman stood up.

"Husband," she said hoarsely. "Where is my boy? Where is Brand?"

"I gave him my sword, Inga," said Hallvard. "I gave him Blood Hunter for his first battle. He will come to no harm."

"He's just a boy!"

"He will not be harmed," Hallvard insisted. "The men will find him."

"But what if they don't?" Inga replied. "If anything happens to him and you could have saved him, you will carry the guilt for the rest of your life."

"And if I leave, and something happens to you and the others here..." Hallvard broke off, the anguish in his voice clear to everyone.

Ragnar stepped forward, his face even older and more solemn in the firelight, but before he could speak, there was a banging at the door. Muffled cries broke out inside the longhouse.

Hallvard strode to the door and flung it open. Thorfinna staggered, gasping, through the door and collapsed to the floor. Her clothes were torn, and her hands and legs were scratched. Tears had streaked through the mud that covered her face.

Inga rushed over to her and grabbed her by the shoulders. "Have you seen Brand?" she cried.

Thorfinna nodded miserably.

"Then where is he?" Inga shook Thorfinna. "Where is he?"

"Inga!" Hallvard barked. "Let the girl catch her breath and speak."

Slowly Thorfinna stood up. "I saw Brand," she said, looking at the floor. "And I saw your brother also," she added, throwing a quick glance in Finn's direction.

"What is it?" cried Inga. "Is he dead? Has he been killed?"

"I don't know," Thorfinna replied. "They were both alive when I saw them last. I was hiding in the trees above the beach. I thought you would want to know how many boats and how many men came. I saw Brand and Arthur in the water. They were walking toward the raiders' longship. Arthur had an ax and Brand had

Blood Hunter, master. I think they meant to sink the ship. There were two raiders on guard, but they didn't see the boys, then the rest of the raiders came running out onto the beach. They ran straight for the boat and the boys had nowhere to hide. The raiders just grabbed them and jumped aboard and started rowing. I ran back here as fast as I could to tell you."

Inga fell against Hallvard and buried her face in his chest. "My poor boy," she whispered. Moments later, the men from the farms arrived back from the beach.

"Gone?" Hallvard barked. They nodded. "You have my thanks, friends," he said, but his eyes glowed with fury as he went on. "They come to raid us in the night. They take my son. And with him, they take my sword..." He broke off and turned slowly to face Finn. "Odin's boy," he growled. "Who are these men? Where will I find them? For when I do, Odin will see such fury in battle as would frighten Thor himself!"

Finn opened his mouth to speak but no words came out. What could he say?

"Speak, boy!" Hallvard bellowed.

"I don't know who they are," Finn stuttered. "I just knew there would be a raid."

"We still don't know that the boy is not a spy," somebody called from the back of the room. Finn recognized Olaf's voice.

"I will vouch for him," said Hallvard. "The boy fought the raiders bravely. He killed grown warriors, and his brother was taken with Brand as they tried to sink the ship."

Finn began breathing again.

"But they have my son, boy." Hallvard leaped forward and grabbed Finn's head in his huge hands. "Odin gave an eye to gain knowledge and see the truth. Maybe if his boy gives an eye, he too will see the truth." He stared into Finn's face. "Call to Odin. Speak to him. Do whatever it is you do, and tell me who these men are!"

"Master, I know who they are," said Thorfinna quietly. All in the room turned toward the girl and saw the rage in her stare. "Their leader is called Moldof."

"How do you know this?" Hallvard demanded. "Did you hear them? Do you know where they live?"

"I did not hear them," she said. "But I saw Moldof. Believe me when I say I know his face all too well."

"Go on, girl," said Hallvard.

"I was born a chieftan's daughter," Thorfinna continued. "You know this."

"And we have treated you well since we bought you," said Inga, sharply.

"That is true," the girl admitted. "Nonetheless, my life now is not the one I thought I was destined for."

"None of us know what the Gods have in store for us," said Hallvard. "But continue. How do you know this Moldof?"

Thorfinna drew a deep breath. "At first we knew him as a troublemaker and a thug. Nobody respected him, but he had a huge family—a clan, really. Then one day, he was accused of murdering one of my kinsmen. We knew that he had killed the man—there were many witnesses and we trusted them. Moldof stabbed the man in the back. It was no honorable fight. It was murder.

"My father sent three men to arrest him, but Moldof overpowered them. He bound their hands and feet, and tortured them. By the time we found them, the bodies were unrecognizable."

Thorfinna paused for a moment and her eyes grew cold.

"Go on, child," said Inga, more gently this time.

Thorfinna took another deep breath and went on, "Moldof and his men came for us that night. They rode into the village, and they killed everyone except for those they could sell as slaves. He said the village was his now. I saw that man kill my father and my mother, and I swore I would never forget his face. The black beard, the dead eyes, the scar on his left cheek. I swore that one day I would find him, and I would watch him die in front of me, just as I watched my parents die. I saw Moldof tonight, master."

Thorfinna broke off, every muscle and sinew in her body taut. The house was silent, except for the crackle and spit of the fire.

Hallvard looked at her thoughtfully. "And could you find your village if you sailed with me?"

"I could," she said at length through clenched teeth. "It is at most two days north along the coast. I used to think about escaping and going back, but where would I go? My family is dead."

"Then we all have reason to find this man. No, not man," Hallvard corrected himself. "This animal. He killed your family. He has taken my son and killed our kinsmen. And he has your brother, Odin's boy."

"What will you do?" Finn asked.

"What will I do? What will we *all* do? We will find them, and we will each of us take back what is ours. We will visit such fury on these people that they never again raid in these parts. Odin's boy, you will come with us. I know we have the Gods on our side, but a little extra help from Odin's messenger would be welcome. Thorfinna, you will be our guide. We sail at dawn." Hallvard looked Thorfinna in the eye. "And we will each have our revenge."

CHAPTER 7

A thin mist hung over the water the next morning as Finn and Thorfinna waited silently on the beach. Behind them stood Ragnar's party from the previous night: wives, children, grandfathers. Finn wanted to say something to Thorfinna, but she had a distant look in her eye as she stared into the mist, and he thought better of it. He shivered, and wrapped the sheepskin he had been given more tightly around his shoulders.

Somebody put a hand on his shoulder, and he turned to see Inga.

"My husband believes that you are Odin's messenger," she said, looking into his eyes. "I do not know. All I know is that you and your brother appeared from nowhere, and the very same night a raiding party came and took my son. So hear me," she went on, her gaze hardening. "If you come back without my son, then I will tear your beating heart from your chest and feed it to the crows. Do you believe me?"

Finn nodded, unable to speak.

"Good," said Inga. "But if indeed you are sent to us from Odin, then know this. Hallvard has the power of Thor, but not always the wisdom of Odin. Brand is the same. And your brother also, perhaps?"

Finn nodded again.

"Then you must be wise for them. All the men will fight with honor, and you too must go with a brave heart. But remember why you are there. The boys—bring them back. Every man dreams of death in battle, but Brand and your brother are too young for Valhalla."

"We won't come back without them," he said, sounding much more certain than he felt.

"Look, now," said Inga, pointing to the trees. "They are coming."

Finn turned and caught his breath. Emerging from the forest onto the beach was a Viking longship. Gliding through the mist on the men's shoulders, it looked too perfect to be real.

The sleek, elegant curve of the prow reared up high in the air like a breaking wave. At the top sat a beautifully carved serpent's head. For the first time since he and Arthur had arrived, and despite the danger that Finn knew he would be sailing toward, he began to feel excited.

The others seemed to feel it, too. Even Thorfinna's eyes burned a little brighter as the men walked into the sea and gently set the boat down in the water alongside a small wooden dock.

The mournful, mist-soaked silence gave way to a clatter of activity. Swift farewells were said, wooden chests were stowed, and the mast was raised and fixed to the hull. Oars scraped and bumped into place. Large, round shields clacked down into their slots along each side of the boat.

Hallvard, standing near the prow, beckoned to Finn. Heart thumping, Finn stepped off the dock and onto the longship with Thorfinna close behind.

"Farewell, Hallvard," cried Inga. "May Thor give you strength in battle. And may Odin guide you to victory. Bring my boy back home. Now, go!"

One of the men still stood on the dock. He leaned against the stern of the ship as it slowly began to slide forward. Then he jumped aboard and sat down in his rowing place. The rowers extended their oars and dipped them into the water. Ragnar stood in the stern of the boat, his hand on the steering oar, and began to call out a beat. The men heaved, their expressions grim, intense, and wild.

Finn watched the people on the dock drift slowly backward, growing smaller and smaller. He turned to Thorfinna, but her icy stare was fixed on something far off.

"Set the sail," cried Ragnar. Two of the men began busying themselves with ropes and a large, red sail began to unfurl. A loud *thwump* drew a cheer from the warriors as the wind filled the sail. The mist grew thinner as the wind grew stronger, and the salt spray splashed across Finn's face. He turned to gaze forward and whisper into the wind, "We're coming for you, Arthur."

Thorfinna looked *at* him instead of *through* him for the first time that day.

"I'm sorry," she said. "You must be worried about your brother. Tell me, what kind of person is he?"

"He's a troublemaker," said Finn. "He loses his temper and picks fights, and doesn't think before he does something. And he thinks he's always right. And he never listens. I wanted to tell him not to go to the beach. I knew there would be raiders guarding the boat and I knew he'd get caught. But he ran off before I could even say a word. He gets himself into these situations, then I have to worry about how to get him out alive."

Thorfinna smiled. "Sounds like most men I know. Is there anything you like about him?"

"He's my brother," Finn snapped. "I love him. That's why I'm here."

Hallvard came up behind them and put a strong hand on Finn's shoulder. "Look at the men in this boat," he said. "Each one of these men will fight to the death under my command. Have no fear. We will find those boys."

Finn looked behind him at the two lines of men. Their fierce eyes, wild grins, huge limbs, and battle-scarred faces were more comforting than anything he had ever seen.

"They won't bring my family back, though," Thorfinna muttered, her expression as dark as the sea.

"And if you see Moldof killed," said Finn carefully, "will that bring them back?"

Thorfinna's eyes flashed like knives. "Tread carefully, Odin's boy. That dog's death will restore honor to my ancestors."

Finn nodded. "I just hope that Moldof doesn't have this hold over you for much longer."

"And what would you do? What would you do if you had seen your entire family murdered by the man who then sold you as a slave?"

Finn thought about all he and Arthur were doing to help the spirit of their great-grandfather finally find peace, and all he was risking to rescue Arthur now. Who could say what they would do if their loved ones had been slaughtered in front of them?

"I hope we all get what we need," he said quietly, but Thorfinna did not hear him. She was staring down into the foaming, heaving sea.

* * *

The sun was dipping into the water at the end of the following day, when Thorfinna announced that they were close to her former home.

"How far?" Hallvard asked.

"We will come to the inlet just beyond the next headland."

After a brief consultation with Ragnar, Hallvard decided that they would find a safe anchorage and wait until dawn before attacking. Ragnar turned the boat toward a small cove. The sail was taken down, the oars placed into the sea once more, and soon the boat was rocking gently in sheltered waters, bounded on three sides by sheer, gray cliffs.

As darkness fell, the men fixed a tent to the edges of the boat and everyone looked for a place to sit that would allow them to sleep as best they could. Salted fish and ale were shared around, and as the men filled their bellies, Hallvard spoke to them.

"Eat well, friends," he began, "for tomorrow we fight. We fight for our honor, we fight for my son, we fight for loot as always, and we fight for Odin, who sent us these two brothers to warn us of the attack."

At this, some of the men began muttering to each other.

"If anyone has anything to say, then let me hear them!" Hallvard shouted, fiercely.

There was a nervous silence, but eventually one of the men spoke up. "Some of us think the boy brings bad luck," he said.

"Bad luck!" roared Hallvard. "He warned us a

raid was coming. Had he not, then my family, and many of yours, would have been slaughtered while we slept. And when the raid came, this *unlucky* boy killed three of the raiders, by my count. Show him some respect. I tell you he speaks for Odin. And his brother—also a mere boy—who alongside my son, tried to sink our enemy's ship. If we fight with half the courage these boys have shown, then victory is certain. Let not another word be spoken against Odin's boy. Now eat. Sleep. And tomorrow we attack!"

"Well said, Hallvard," Ragnar cried out from the back of the ship. "A cheer for Odin's boy!" The men cheered and laughed, and Hallvard thumped Finn on the back. Finn smiled with pride in the darkness.

Later, as he settled down to sleep, in the bottom

of the boat, Hallvard called over to him, "What will you dream of, Odin's boy?"

"I will dream about my brother," he replied.

"And I will dream about my son," said Hallvard.

"And I will dream of revenge," whispered Thorfinna.

EXTRACT FROM *WARRIOR HEROES*
BY FINN BLADE

VIKING LONGSHIPS

Vikings do lots of things well. They are very good at fighting, drinking, and telling stories. But if there's one thing they do better than anything else, it has to be building and sailing ships. So what's so good about a Viking longship?

- You can sail it across an ocean. Vikings have sailed through icebergs to Greenland, and across the Atlantic to North America.

- You can scare the living daylights out of people with the monster figurehead that sits at the top of the prow. The blood-red sail only adds to the effect.

- When you get to the other side of the ocean, you can land on a beach or row up a river. The lowest point of a longship sits only about 3 feet (1 meter) below the water.

- If anyone attacks the boat, you can just keep rowing. Your shield fits into a slot along the top edge (gunwale) of the boat, protecting you from arrows.

- If you need to take an overland shortcut to speed things up, then your ship is light enough that you and your fellow sailor-warriors can lift it out of the water and carry it.

- If you need to get away quickly, or if you suddenly spot an iceberg, you can reverse easily.

The front and rear of the ship
are almost perfectly symmetrical.

- And last but not least, everyone
  is so scared of how fierce you
  are and so sure that your boat
  is faster, that if you are about
  to attack, then the enemy will be
  expecting to lose!

CHAPTER 8

"It's time," said Ragnar at first light. The men in the ship began to stir and rub cramped limbs after a fitful night's sleep. Finn stretched and stood up, letting out a long yawn. The tent came down as quickly as it had gone up. Food was passed around as Hallvard addressed the men.

"Each of you, check your weapons now. Be ready. We will beach the ship out of sight of the village. Thorfinna knows the shore here well. We plan to take Moldof by surprise, but we may be seen. Remember, as soon as we are clear of this anchorage, be prepared to fight at any time."

The men reached into their sea chests and withdrew an array of swords, axes, knives, and spears. Hallvard turned to Thorfinna and Finn, holding out two bows and two quivers full of arrows.

"May your aim be as true today as it was a few nights ago," he said to Finn. He reached down and handed over a pair of swords and shields. "Take these, also," he said. "Do not rush into the battle. You are both brave, but you are both young, and I hope you will not need to use them."

Thorfinna's expression as she snatched the weapons suggested that she felt differently.

"We all know what we need to do," Hallvard shouted. "May all of us fight well, and any of us that fall be taken by the Valkyries to feast in Valhalla. Ragnar, take us to battle!"

They made swift progress around the headland. The sun had not yet risen as they pulled into a long inlet under Thorfinna's guidance. Soon enough, Thorfinna had directed Ragnar toward a thin strip of beach. The men stopped rowing and jumped into the water to drag the boat onto the sand.

"No sign of a welcome party," said Hallvard. "Thorfinna, the village is near?"

"We will see it from the top of that ridge behind the beach," she replied, her voice strained.

"Ten minutes on foot."

"Good," said Hallvard, briskly. "Men, make ready. Ragnar, Finn, Thorfinna—with me."

Shields strapped to their backs, Finn and Thorfinna followed Ragnar and Hallvard as they strode across the sand and bounded up the rocks.

"Is this the place?" Hallvard asked, pointing along the coast to a collection of ten or so houses next to another strip of sand. A longship was moored to a jetty a short way from the houses.

Thorfinna nodded, her face pure white. "Yes, and that is the ship that Brand and Arthur tried to sink."

Ragnar and Hallvard stared at the village. It lay on the shore at the bottom of a wooded valley, on one side of which the hills sloped steeply down to the shore. On the other side, the hills ended abruptly at a small cliff overlooking the sea and the village.

"Thorfinna," said Ragnar. "It seems to me that if we want to get close and stay hidden, we should approach from the trees on the hill. Is that correct?"

She nodded again, not taking her eyes off the village.

Hallvard turned to Ragnar. "What are your thoughts?"

"We must cut off Moldof's escape," the old man replied. "Otherwise, he could make off with the boys when we attack."

"Two groups, then?"

Ragnar nodded.

"I agree," said Hallvard, decisively. "You will

lead a small party and conceal yourselves as best you can along the path at the bottom of the valley. I will lead the main group and attack from the hill."

"One more thing, Hallvard." Ragnar looked worried.

"What is it?"

"We are not certain that Moldof is here," said Ragnar, thoughtfully.

"That is the ship," Thorfinna hissed. "He's there."

"We must be certain," Ragnar insisted. "If we are wrong, we will be starting a war. I have an idea," he went on. "I suggest that Finn and Thorfinna take a position on top of the rocks that overlook the village. As soon as Thorfinna sees someone that she is sure serves Moldof, then she and Odin's boy begin shooting. That is our signal to attack."

"Agreed," said Hallvard. "It's settled."

Hallvard turned and waved to the men back on the beach. Finn's chest tightened as they ran forward. Several of the men had painted their faces. They looked more like gods and monsters than men.

"Look!" cried Thorfinna. Finn turned in time to see some rocks tumbling down to the water a short distance from the village.

"Did you see anyone?" Hallvard asked quickly.

"I don't know for sure, master," said Thorfinna. "I thought I saw someone in the trees."

"Quiet, everyone," Ragnar hissed. The whole group froze, straining to catch any sound that might signal someone running. There was nothing.

"We must move forward," said Hallvard. Quietly, he explained the plan to the men as they walked up to the trees and began the march toward the village.

They had not walked far before Thorfinna turned impatiently to Hallvard. "Master, Finn and I should go ahead, as we have the farthest to go."

"Agreed," replied the Viking warrior. "Remember, Finn, we will be waiting for your signal."

"Yes, sir," said Finn.

"Come on," Thorfinna urged. With Finn close behind, she began running silently through the trees. It was hard going, weighed down by the huge shields, sheepskins, and weapons. Before long, Finn was whispering hoarsely to Thorfinna to stop. She turned impatiently.

"The longer we take, the more likely it is that Moldof will know we are here," she said. "We can't keep stopping."

Finn nodded, holding a hand up as he stooped to catch his breath. A stick snapped a short way ahead of them. Finn's eyes widened and they both froze.

Silence.

Thorfinna beckoned Finn on. The path began to lead downhill, and a few minutes later, Thorfinna held up her hand and stopped again. Relieved for the pause, Finn gasped for air. Ahead lay a break in the trees. Finn realized it must be the main path along the bottom of the valley toward the village. Thorfinna scurried across the path and back into the trees on the other side.

Glancing both ways and seeing nothing, Finn dashed after her. He had just reached the cover of the trees when another stick snapped, this time behind them. They spun around. Nothing.

"What if we're being followed?" Finn whispered.

"Nothing we can do," Thorfinna replied. "If there's someone tracking us, we can't see them. And they haven't attacked us."

Finn wasn't so sure. "Should we at least wait for Ragnar's men to warn them that Moldof may know we're here?"

Thorfinna shook her head. "We can't change the plan. Hallvard needs us on top of the cliff to signal when to attack. Come on." She turned and ran ahead. Not wanting to be left behind, Finn followed immediately.

They ran uphill, Finn's chest burning as he

took in great gulps of cold air. Finally, to Finn's almost tearful relief, Thorfinna slowed to a walk.

"Nearly there," she whispered, crouching down as she turned off the path. They walked downhill toward the sea until they reached the edge of the trees.

"We should stay hidden," Finn whispered.

Peering down through the lowest branches, they had a perfect view of the village, and beyond that, the hill from which Hallvard planned to attack.

Thorfinna frowned.

"What is it?" Finn asked.

"They know we're here," she said. "I can feel it. Look. There's smoke coming from the houses, and there are roosters crowing, but nobody is outside. Something's wrong." She turned to Finn.

"You stay here. I'm going to warn Hallvard."

"Wait!" Finn hissed. "A few minutes ago you were saying we couldn't change the plan. What if you get caught? What will Moldof do to you this time?"

"This time, I've got *this*," she said, brandishing her sword. "And the next time I see that animal, I will split his festering heart in two." She held the sword in both hands, her knuckles white and her jaw stiff. "I pity the fool who tries to stop me," she spat. Finn dared not argue any further, as Thorfinna turned and disappeared back into the trees.

The minutes crept by and Finn, alone for the first time since Arthur's capture, began to dwell on what might have become of his brother. As hard as he tried to concentrate on the village below, Finn was plagued by visions of Arthur and Brand being tormented by Moldof's men. Thorfinna had spoken about Moldof's barbaric treatment of her family. What if the same fate had befallen Arthur? The thought twisted Finn's gut into a knot.

By the time a quarter of an hour or so had passed, he was seething. How was he supposed to signal to Hallvard if he didn't know who Moldof's men were? And how would he know that without Thorfinna telling him? *She's as bad as Arthur,* he thought, as he stared down at the village. Finn tried to imagine the Professor sitting beside him. He knew what the old man would have said: "Stay where you are, old chap, and follow orders. You can't win this one on your own."

And that was when strong arms grabbed Finn from behind. A rough hand clamped itself firmly over his mouth to muffle his cries. He kicked and writhed around, but was completely powerless to resist being dragged backward. He heard the metallic scrape of a sword being drawn.

Finn's blood ran cold, then someone whispered, "Not yet. He's more use alive. For now..."

CHAPTER 9

A cloth was stuffed into Finn's mouth to gag him, his hands were tied behind his back, and a rope was looped around his waist. Then he was spun around, and his heart sank as he saw his captors for the first time. Two huge warriors flanked their cruel-looking leader.

"I wonder..." said the leader, running a hand

across his black beard and scarred cheek. "Do you know who I am?"

Finn shook his head, wanting to give nothing away.

"Really? My name is Moldof."

Finn shook his head again.

"A boy sent to do a man's work," mused Moldof. "Strange. Two boys tried to attack my ship on my last raid. And now another boy spies on my village. Strange, strange, strange. Perhaps you know my thralls?"

Moldof flashed a quick grin at Finn and waved to one of his men. "Ulf," said Moldof, never taking his eyes off Finn, "I think our new friend would like to meet the thralls."

One of the warriors laughed and strode back up the hill.

Moldof went on. "Early in the morning, my scouts come to me. They tell me that a strange ship sails in from the sea, ready for battle. When they land, the warriors from the ship creep toward my village, hiding in the trees so that they can attack by surprise. I wonder what it is they want?"

Ulf returned, leading two cloaked figures on a rope.

"Take their hoods off," said Moldof, his cold eyes still on Finn.

Finn knew what he was going to see, but as the two hoods were thrown back to reveal two more gagged faces, his shoulders sagged in surrender. Brand and Arthur stared back at him, looking thoroughly miserable.

"Just as I thought," said Moldof. "Now, there's

something you should all see." He grabbed the ropes that led from the boys' waists and yanked them toward the top of the cliff, bringing them to a stop where Finn and Thorfinna had been waiting moments earlier, just hidden from the village in the trees.

To Finn's horror he saw that Hallvard and his men had emerged from hiding. There was still no sign of life in the village. Hallvard had evidently grown tired of waiting. Crouched and alert, Hallvard's men advanced toward the houses.

"I am Hallvard Forkbeard," the huge warrior's voice rang out. "I seek my son and his captor, Moldof. Show yourself!"

Moldof laughed menacingly.

"Show yourself and fight like a man!" Hallvard

thundered on his shield with his ax.

Moldof stepped forward to the top of the cliff. "Up here!" he yelled. At that moment, the doors of several houses burst open, and suddenly the village was full of men, roaring terrible war cries.

The boys watched in horror as a savage battle played out in front of them. Screams of fear and pain mixed with bellows of anger as the men fought, attacking each other brutally. Not one showed mercy.

It was impossible for the boys to tell who was winning. There were no uniforms or flags, only huge warriors slaughtering and being slaughtered. But soon enough, the balance of power became obvious. Men that Finn did not recognize began to turn and run, pursued by men he did recognize from the ship.

Hallvard turned to look up at the cliff top once more and roared, but the sound died in his throat when he saw Moldof pull the boys out from the trees and push them toward the edge of the cliff.

"Brand!" Hallvard cried, through the din of the groans of the dying. As he stood staring up at his son on the cliff, his legs suddenly crumpled and he fell to his knees. His ax and shield fell from his hands. He had not seen the injured man beside him bring out his knife. He seemed to ignore the knife as it slid into his back. He barely moved as Ragnar came to his aid, spearing his assailant.

The three boys stood at the top of the precipice looking down to the lethal rocks at the base of the cliff. Finn looked over at Moldof and saw him grinning insanely. The cruel warrior put his hands around Brand's neck, and lifted him off his feet to dangle over the drop. Brand kicked frantically, and Moldof started to laugh again.

The sound was drowned out by a blood-curdling scream of pure rage. The boys saw Moldof's man Ulf stagger forward and topple over the edge of the cliff, an ax protruding from his back. Moldof dropped Brand, who just managed to grab on to a corner of rock. He hung precariously from the top of the cliff.

Arthur rushed to help him up. Another scream of rage tore through the air. Finn turned to see Thorfinna kicking a man to the ground. He shuddered as she pulled her sword from the man's stomach. Her eyes were round with fury and her mouth flecked with foam as she turned to face Moldof. He circled her warily, sword drawn.

"I remember you, girl," he sneered. "I remember your parents, also."

Thorfinna seemed not to hear him. It was as though she were possessed. She flew at him, sword swinging, smashing blows down on him that seemed impossibly powerful for someone her size.

Surprised, Moldof was driven backward to the cliff. Thorfinna lunged with her shield and caught Moldof square in the mouth. He staggered a short step backward, catching his heel and beginning to topple. He dropped his sword and groaned.

Letting out a final terrible scream, Thorfinna drove her sword into Moldof's chest, then let go.

With a look of shock, Moldof fell backward off the cliff and plunged to the rocks below.

Thorfinna stared down at his motionless body and snarled. Then she picked up the sword Moldof had dropped and turned to the boys. Each of them flinched as she stepped toward them, still wide-eyed with rage. She sliced through the ropes that tied them, and threw

Moldof's sword to the ground at Brand's feet. Her face full of fury, Thorfinna turned and rushed back toward the path.

The boys removed their gags and stared at one another, pale and shaking their heads.

"We're still alive," said Finn.

"We were saved by a slave," said Arthur.

"Not just a slave—a berserker," said Brand, stooping down to pick up the sword. He looked at it fondly.

"Blood Hunter," he breathed. "Arthur, Finn— with me. We must join the battle!"

Before they had taken a step, Ragnar burst from the trees and seized Brand's arm.

"It is over, the victory is ours!" he cried. "But you must come now. Your father has fallen. He does not have long to live."

EXTRACT FROM *WARRIOR HEROES* BY FINN BLADE

RAIDERS AND BERSERKERS

The point of raiding started out simply as a way of stealing as much treasure as possible from a village, before returning home to the farm. It was a summertime activity that usually involved a group of men in one boat. In fact, the word Viking probably means "pirate" in Norse, the Vikings' own language. These raids became feared all over Europe because the Vikings fought fiercely.

Raids eventually became more organized. The Vikings began to sail many boats up rivers to attack entire cities. They attacked and killed anyone who got in their way, then took control of the city. They stole whatever they could find. Then they demanded huge payments of gold and silver from the most powerful ruler in return for leaving the city. People were so afraid of Viking warriors, that they usually paid up.

The most feared of all Viking warriors were the berserkers. They wore bearskins or wolfskins instead of armor. Before going into battle, they whipped themselves into an eye-rolling, mouth-foaming frenzy, and did crazy things such as biting chunks out of their shields. Witnesses said that the berserkers fought with superhuman strength and did not feel pain, even from sword edges or fire.

Some say that berserkers are Odin's own warriors, and he gives them this superhuman strength.

CHAPTER 10

Ragnar led the boys down to the village. The ground was strewn with the bodies of dying men, silenced forever. All of Moldof's men had either fled or been killed. Several of Hallvard's men lay dead, too, and the rest were clustered around their fallen leader. They stepped aside as Ragnar and the boys approached.

"Father," cried Brand, rushing forward to kneel

at Hallvard's side. "This is my fault. If I had not–"

Hallvard held up a hand to silence him.

"My son," he began, weakly. "We should be rejoicing."

"How can I rejoice when you lie dying?" Brand sobbed.

"I die on the battlefield, victorious," said Hallvard. "I die with honor, and I die knowing that Valhalla awaits. I die knowing that my son carries my sword, Blood Hunter. And I die knowing that my family is saved. You will join me one day, boy. But first, you must

become a great warrior." He paused, breathing very heavily now. "Promise me three things, my son," he went on.

"Anything, Father."

"Look after your mother, Brand. You are the head of the family now."

"Of course I will, Father," said Brand tearfully.

"Look after Blood Hunter," Hallvard continued. "That sword has brought many great victories to me, and my father before me. Use it well."

"Yes, Father."

"And the last thing..." Hallvard tried to sit up, but he groaned and collapsed back again. He lay silent for a few moments, breathing heavily and gathering his remaining strength.

"My time has nearly come, Brand," Hallvard resumed. "The last thing you must promise me is this: Thorfinna must be set free, for she is no thrall. It was she who led us to you, and it was she who killed Moldof. Free her, Brand."

"I will, Father."

"Master!" Thorfinna had joined the group unnoticed. The wild look had left her face. She looked utterly exhausted, as she knelt down beside Brand.

"Ah, here she is," whispered Hallvard. "And Odin's boys, where are they?"

Finn and Arthur stepped forward.

"You have all fought bravely, like true warriors. You have helped me to save my son and my honor. And because of you, I die happy and ready for Valhalla. My thanks could never be enough. I will be waiting for all of you." Hallvard reached up and grasped Brand's hand.

He smiled, and closed his eyes.

Brand remained at his father's side, holding his hand. "Feast well in Valhalla, Hallvard Forkbeard," he whispered. "You will be honored there for all time."

When he stood to address the group, Brand seemed to have aged a decade.

"My thanks to all you men who fought so bravely alongside my father," he said. "I hope that when it is needed, I will lead you to many more victories." He pointed Blood Hunter to the sky, and threw back his head. "Odin, hear me! Give me the courage to honor Hallvard in battle. Give me the strength to wield his sword and bring these men victory in his name and yours. Give me the wisdom to lead as he did!"

Brand lowered the sword, and his voice

wavered as he went on. "But for now, we must take his body back to my mother."

Seeing the anguish on the boy's face, Ragnar said softly, "She will be proud that he died in battle to save you, Brand."

Brand nodded, blinking back the tears that threatened to overtake him. "My father's final wish is one we can honor immediately." He turned to the girl who had lived with his family as a thrall for so long.

"Thorfinna, who fought with the strength of ten men, you have brought honor to your family by killing the murderer who slew your mother and father. My father's dying wish was that you should be freed, and this shall be done at once. You may return with me and live in freedom as part of my family, or you may follow your own path. Which do you choose?"

Thorfinna looked around at the bodies covering the ground. She gazed at the houses in the village she had once called home, turned back to Brand.

"I will stay by your side," she said. "But on one condition."

"Name it," said Brand. Thorfinna smiled for the first time since Moldof's attack in the night.

"You will take me with you whenever you go raiding."

"Then it is decided," said Brand. He placed a hand on Thorfinna's shoulder. "After your performance this morning, I would have you fight alongside me as soon as any man."

The other men nodded approvingly.

"And what of Odin's boys?" Brand went on, turning to Finn and Arthur. "What will you do now? Your warning saved us all. You, too, are welcome to stay with us."

Arthur and Finn looked at one another and smiled.

"I think we've done what we came here to do," said Arthur.

"Odin has many uses for us, and we will make our own way from here," Finn added. "We are never able to stay in one place for long."

"I thought that might be your answer," said Brand. "It has been an honor to fight at your side. May Odin continue to grant you the wisdom and courage you brought with you."

"Now men," Brand continued. "We must take the bodies back home."

While the group set about their grim task, Thorfinna came over to Finn and touched his arm.

"Thank you," she said softly.

"What for?" Finn asked.

"Brand is right. Without your warning, we all would have died. Instead, most of us live, and I have kept my oath to avenge the murder of my family."

"And you are now a free woman, as promised," said Arthur.

"Thank you both," she said again, then turned to follow the men as they carried their dead back to the boat, ready to set to sea once more.

Finn and Arthur looked at one another. They knew their job was done. Thorfinna had been freed, Blood Hunter had been returned to its rightful owner, and Hallvard's spirit had begun the journey to Valhalla.

Looking around them, they became aware of a thickening sea mist. The white vapor swirled gracefully around them, until they could no longer see one another.

As the mist slowly cleared, Finn and Arthur began to make out the familiar shapes and smells of the Professor's study. Standing tall and imposing as ever, the huge figure of Hallvard's ghost faded with the mist, until it had vanished completely.

WARRIOR HEROES
The Knight's Enemies
Benjamin Hulme-Cross

Forced to travel back in time by the terrifying ghost
of Sir William Mallory, can brothers Arthur and
Finn prevent the death of his daughter and stop
the castle falling? Will the boys escape after being
captured and imprisoned, succeed in changing the
course of history, and make it back to the present?

Extract from
WARRIOR HEROES
The Knight's Enemies

Arthur became aware of a steady, far-off roar, like the sea heard from a distance. His mind reached out toward the sound and it grew louder. He blinked his eyes against the darkness, but he could still see nothing. Gradually, he began to make out more sounds intermingled with the roar. He realized they were shouts, though they still sounded distant. *Where am I?* he wondered, noticing for the first time how cold he was. The air around him began to move, and he had the strange sensation that he was falling backward.

Shadowy figures appeared in front of a shimmering light before him. It was only as his mouth filled with icy water that he realized he was looking up at the sky. *I'm underwater,* he thought calmly. Then he awoke. Suddenly terrified, he thrashed around in the water. His foot struck something hard, and he kicked up toward daylight.

Chest burning, he shot up through the water. He broke the surface, gulping in a huge, spluttering lungful of air. He twisted around to the sound of shouting and saw that he was in a fast-flowing river. A steep, rocky bank was slipping quickly by in a blur of green.

"Quick, boy!" someone yelled.

The water spun Arthur around as it whisked him along. To his horror, he saw that he was fast approaching a watermill. Its giant paddles churned slowly through water that swirled and bubbled ominously.

He kicked and thrashed toward the bank, and his hand brushed against a stone. It was worn smooth by the river and he slid helplessly on.

"Help!" Arthur cried, swallowing mouthfuls of icy water. The paddles churned closer and closer.

"Here, boy! You only have one chance." A man sprinting along the bank next to Arthur soon pulled ahead and stood in between him and the mill. The man reached down and held a long staff over the water. Arthur bobbed toward the staff, twisting desperately to position himself. A moment later, he had it in both hands. His head dipped below the water as the current tugged him around. One hand slipped off the staff, and he felt the other beginning to slide. As the creak of the mill got louder, Arthur closed his eyes.

About the author

Growing up in London I spent a lot of time sitting on the Underground, daydreaming and reading books. Historical adventures in far-flung lands were always my favorite, and I used to love visiting castles and ruins.

After I left home, I lived in Japan for a while and learned all about the Samurai. Now I've swapped the city for the countryside, and as well as reading books I also write stories and plays for young people.

The thing I like most about being a writer is playing around with ideas for stories in my head—which is daydreaming really, so not much has changed!